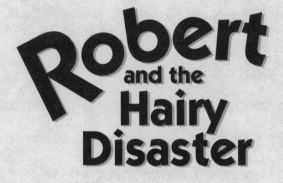

Robert
and the
Hairy
Disaster

**Also by Barbara Seuling**

# Robert
### and the
## Hairy
## Disaster

## by Barbara Seuling
## Illustrated by Paul Brewer

**A**
**LITTLE APPLE**
**PAPERBACK**

SCHOLASTIC INC.

New York  Toronto  London  Auckland  Sydney
Mexico City  New Delhi  Hong Kong  Buenos Aires

ISBN 0-439-35378-5

12  11  10  9  8  7  6  5  4  3          2  3  4  5  6/0

Printed in the U.S.A.
First Scholastic printing, September 2002

# Contents

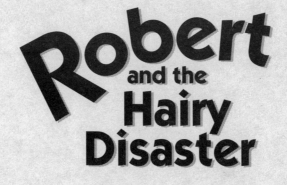

# Back-to-school Special

**R**obert unbuckled his seat belt and hopped out of the car. "Come on, Paul." His best friend, Paul, jumped out right behind him.

"Wait up, guys," said Robert's mom, locking the car door. "There's no need to rush. School doesn't start until Monday."

The boys slowed down as they headed for the automatic doors. Mrs. Dorfman followed behind them.

They passed right by the mall directory. They knew exactly where they were going

1

first—to the pet store. Robert had to buy food for Fuzzy, his pet tarantula, and a chew stick for Trudy, the class hamster. He couldn't wait to see her again after a whole summer off. Abby Ranko had gotten to take her home this time. Robert hoped she had remembered to give Trudy chew sticks.

The pet shop was at the other end of the mall. Robert bought the tarantula food and the chew stick. Next was the drug-store, with its special back-to-school sale on paper and pens and other supplies. Robert bought a fat notebook with a dog

on the cover. Paul got one with a picture of a rocket being launched.

When they were finished shopping, Mrs. Dorfman asked if they were hungry.

"I'm starving," said Robert, heading for the escalator. The smells of pizza, hamburgers, fries, tacos, hot dogs, pretzels, and stuffed baked potatoes filled the air.

"Me, too," said Paul, following Robert up the last few steps to the food court.

They all had hamburgers and fries. "Did you get everything you need?" asked Mrs. Dorfman. Robert nodded as he dipped a fry into a puddle of ketchup. Paul nodded, too, his mouth full.

They left the food court and walked toward the exit. As they passed Ernesto's Hair Emporium, Mrs. Dorfman stopped.

"Robert, we should get you a haircut while we're here," Mrs. Dorfman said.

They were having a back-to-school special, too.

Oh, no. Robert hated getting haircuts at the mall. The barber, Ernesto, always teased him about his curly hair. Once he said, "My daughter would love to have curls like these." Robert had wanted to slide under the chair.

"Mom, can't we wait? It's our last Saturday before school starts. Paul and I want to ride our bikes." He looked at Paul.

"Oh," said Paul, surprised. "Yeah."

"They do look pretty busy," said Mrs. Dorfman. "Maybe we can come back during the week."

Robert rolled his eyes in relief. Paul smiled as they headed for the exit again.

# First Day of School

The air was buzzing around him as Robert walked into the classroom. The first day of school was always exciting. It was fun to see the other kids and Mrs. Bernthal again, and the class pets, too.

He sat down at his usual place—Table Four—with Paul and Vanessa. From his seat, he could look right across at Susanne Lee Rodgers, the smartest girl in the class, at Table Three.

Mrs. Bernthal welcomed them all back to school. "Aren't we lucky to be together again?" she said. "You may take a few minutes to get reacquainted." Chairs scraped the floor as children got up and moved around.

Robert loved Mrs. Bernthal. She was always kind and cheerful, and never made anyone feel stupid. She had even given the class a present. She had brought them a two-foot-long green ribbon snake. They had named her Sally. "This is for being the best class in the whole school," Mrs. Bernthal had said.

Robert went to the back of the room where the animals were kept. There was Sally, all smooth and pretty, resting on her cedar chips and twigs as always.

"Hi, Sally," said Robert, reaching in to stroke her slim green body with his finger. She wiggled into an S-curve.

The class was still buzzing as kids said hello to each other and showed off their new sneakers or book bags.

After a while, Robert took the chew stick out of his pocket and went over to Trudy's cage. Trudy wasn't there. Puzzled, he looked around for Abby Ranko. She was at her table, talking to Matt Blakey and Brian Hoberman. Robert walked over.

"Hi, Abby," he said. "Hi, Matt. Hi, Brian."

"Hi, Robert," said Abby. The boys just grunted.

"Um, I was wondering," said Robert. "You took Trudy home over the summer vacation, didn't you?"

Abby nodded.

"Where is she?"

Abby looked down. "I'm sorry," she said in a soft little voice. "Trudy's dead."

Robert gasped. He felt as though he had been punched in the stomach. He went back to his table.

"Trudy's dead," he told Paul, sliding into his chair.

"Oh, no," said Paul. He shook his head sadly. "Poor old Trudy."

Yeah. Things did not look great, and this was only the beginning of the first day of school.

# Different

**R**obert and Paul slid into their usual lunchroom seats. Robert opened his sandwich and began picking the salami out of it.

"You look different." It was Susanne Lee Rodgers. Robert didn't have to turn around to know that. Her voice made Robert grind his teeth.

"I'm the same," he said to her, closing up his sandwich again.

"Hmmm," said Susanne Lee. "I don't think so." She walked away to join Vanessa

Nicolini and Emily Asher. They always sat
together at lunch.

"Do I look different to you?" Robert asked
Paul. Paul looked at him over his tomato-
and-cheese sandwich. "Uh-uh," he said.

*What is Susanne Lee talking about?* Robert wondered. *What could be different about me?*

Over at Susanne Lee's lunch table, Vanessa and Emily giggled. Robert was sure it was about him. He looked down the front of his shirt. He checked his zipper. They were both okay.

Back in the classroom, there were more giggles. Robert excused himself and took the pass to go to the boys' room. He felt the seat of his pants. It was not torn. He checked his shoes. There was no toilet paper trailing from them. He looked in the mirror.

There was nothing gross on his face or between his teeth. He looked closely at one eye, then the other. He saw a couple of freckles on his nose he didn't remember. Could that be it? He leaned over the sink and stuck his tongue way out. It looked like his regular tongue.

The door opened and Brian walked in. He stared at Robert.

"Hi," he said.

Robert muttered, "Hi," and hurried back to the classroom.

First Trudy and now this. Robert wished he could start the day all over again.

# Summer Vacation

After lunch, they settled down again at their tables. Mrs. Bernthal took a piece of chalk and wrote SUMMER VACATION on the chalkboard.

"Did anyone do anything special this summer?" she asked.

Joey Rizzo raised his hand. Mrs. Bernthal called on him.

"My dad took me to a baseball game at Yankee Stadium."

Mrs. Bernthal wrote BASEBALL on the chalkboard. "What can you tell us about it?" she asked.

"We had hot dogs and soda," said Joey.

"Anything else?"

Joey thought for a minute. "Oh," he said. "Yeah. And peanuts."

"Very nice, Joey," said Mrs. Bernthal.

Susanne Lee raised her hand.

"Yes, Susanne Lee. Tell us what you did on your summer vacation."

"I went to the American Museum of Natural History in New York City," she said. Mrs. Bernthal wrote MUSEUMS on the board. Susanne Lee described the dinosaur exhibit. "One skeleton is so big it takes up almost the whole room," she said. Robert felt a little jealous. He wished he could have seen that exhibit.

Abby raised her hand.

"Abby, tell us about your summer vacation," said Mrs. Bernthal.

Abby got up slowly. "I want to tell you about Trudy," she said in a tiny voice. The class got very quiet.

"One day I went to feed her," she said, "and she wasn't moving. I was scared. I called my mom. My mom looked at Trudy and said she was dead." Abby sniffled a little as she spoke.

"I cried. I told my mom I fed her and gave her water every day and cleaned her cage once a week. She said Trudy probably just died of old age. I cried anyway. I was afraid no one in the class would like me anymore. They would think I killed Trudy."

Robert felt a lump in his throat. He *had* been a little mad at Abby when he found out about Trudy. Now he felt sorry for her. It could have happened to anyone, even him. He imagined how terrible he would feel if Trudy had died while he was taking care of her.

Abby sat down. Robert saw Pamela Rose lean over to Abby and whisper something.

Emily Asher was next, talking about her family's trip to visit relatives in North Carolina.

Later, they got into groups to work on math. Robert was in the same group as Abby.

"You were a very good hamster monitor," he told her. "And everyone still likes you." He went back to his math problem. Then he said, "What did you do with her?"

"We buried her in the backyard," Abby said. "In a cookie box."

Robert smiled. "That's nice," he said. "Trudy loved cookies."

Abby smiled for the first time that day.

# The Haircut

When the bell rang, Robert and Paul grabbed their book bags and jackets and left together. Giggles came from behind them. It was Susanne Lee and Emily. What was so funny? Paul just shrugged, but Robert was really bothered by it.

They walked to Robert's house to do their homework. Suddenly, Robert realized what the problem must be. His hair! His mother had told him he needed a haircut. Why hadn't he listened? He opened the front door with his key. Nobody else was home yet. They went upstairs to Robert's room.

"You've got to do me a big favor," he said to Paul.

Paul sat in the beanbag chair they used for all their important thinking. "Sure. What?"

"I need you to cut my hair," said Robert.

"No way!" said Paul, jumping up. "I don't know how to cut hair!"

"You've got to. It's a matter of life and death, almost. I won't go back to school tomorrow unless my hair is cut. Everyone is laughing at me. If I tell my mom, she'll make me go to Ernesto's. You've got to help me. You're my best friend."

Robert opened his desk drawer and took out a pair of scissors. He held them out to Paul.

Paul took the scissors from Robert. He looked miserable. Reluctantly, he started snipping. He snipped there, he snipped here. *Snip, snip, snip.* Robert was getting more fidgety every moment. Finally, he couldn't stand the suspense any longer.

"Well? What's happening? How does it look?"

"I—I don't know," said Paul.

Uh-oh. That didn't sound good.

Robert jumped up and ran to the bathroom mirror. His hair looked like a lunar landscape. Bumps. Holes. Uneven.

"Oh, no!" he cried.

"I told you I didn't know how to do this!" Robert saw that Paul was really upset.

The door downstairs slammed. That must be his brother, Charlie. Robert tried not to panic.

"It's fine," he told Paul, even though it wasn't.

"Really?" said Paul.

Robert felt his head. He gulped. "Sure. It's not so bad."

Paul packed up his things. "I have to go," he said.

"I'm sorry, Paul," said Robert. "I shouldn't have asked you to cut my hair."

"It's okay," said Paul.

After Paul left, Robert had to think fast.

His dad would be home soon. Feeling desperate, Robert went to Charlie's room. Although Charlie sometimes teased him, once in a while he was okay.

"What's up?" asked Charlie, his earphones hanging around his neck.

"Can you help me?" asked Robert.

Charlie looked up and laughed. "What happened to you?"

"It's not important. I just need you to fix it for me. Can you?"

Charlie stared at Robert. "Fix it? You want me to fix that mess?"

Robert gulped. "Yeah."

Charlie hesitated. "Okay. Sure." He grinned. "Come over here and sit down." Robert did as he was told.

Charlie fished around on his desk for a pair of scissors. "This should be easy," he said. He started clipping. Robert saw chunks of hair falling to the floor.

"Not too short!" he said.

"The only way to fix this is to get it real short, like mine," said Charlie. "Hold still."

Charlie had a buzz cut. Robert hated buzz cuts. He ran away before one more chunk of hair fell.

"What're you doing?" cried Charlie.

In the bathroom, Robert looked in the mirror and groaned. The hair on one side of his head was much shorter than the hair on the other.

"What am I going to do?" he said. If Susanne Lee thought he looked different before, what would she think now?

He ran to his room, closed the door, and locked it. He would just stay in there until his hair grew out.

# Lumpy and Bumpy

"**R**obert, I'm not going to call you again. Come down to dinner NOW."

Robert's parents had been coaxing him to come downstairs to eat dinner for half an hour. This time he heard his dad's "no more nonsense" voice. Robert had held out as long as he could. He would have to go downstairs to eat dinner with his family.

*Thump, thump, thump.* He thumped down the stairs in his sneakers and slid into his seat at the table. He wore the over-the-head rubber monster mask his dad had given him last Halloween.

"Robert, what on earth is that?" cried his mother.

"It's my Halloween mask," said Robert. It sounded more like "Im eye allowee mack."

"Take that thing off, Robert," his father ordered.

"I have to get used to it for Halloween," said Robert. It sounded like "I happto getchooz tootfor allowee."

"Halloween is still a long way off," said his father.

"Yes, Robert. Take it off. It's not healthy. You'll smother. Besides, you won't be able to eat your dinner." Mrs. Dorfman piled spaghetti onto Robert's plate.

Charlie jumped in. "It has holes for breathing," he said. "You can suck spaghetti right through the mouth hole. Show them, Robert." He lifted a strand of spaghetti off Robert's plate and stuck it through the mouth hole. With a long *shluuuuuuuurrrrrp,* the spaghetti disappeared.

It was good to have Charlie sticking up for him. Of course, Charlie was probably just protecting himself. After all, Charlie had played a part in this haircut disaster.

"That's it, Robert," said Mr. Dorfman firmly. "Remove that thing at once."

Slowly, Robert removed the mask. Mr. Dorfman's mouth fell open. Mrs. Dorfman let out a high-pitched squeak. Charlie couldn't help himself. He roared with laughter.

"I think we need an explanation," said Mr. Dorfman. The vein in his neck was throbbing.

Robert cleared his throat. "Everyone was laughing at me," he said. "I had to do something."

"Why would they laugh at you?" asked his mother, stifling her own laughter.

"I thought it was probably my hair," he said.

"What was wrong with your hair?" said his father, who was beginning to laugh, too.

"It looked funny." Robert stared at the mound of spaghetti in front of him.

Usually, he loved spaghetti, but now it might just as well be a plate full of worms.

"It did not look funny, Robert. It was just a little long. I knew we should have seen Ernesto on Saturday." His mom tried to reassure him, but soon everyone was laughing.

"You can't go to school like that," his mother continued. "Your hair is lumpy and bumpy. You look . . ."

"Deranged?" offered Charlie.

"No. That's not what I was going to say. You look . . . well . . . sort of . . . unfinished. And Ernesto's is closed now. I'll have to fix it myself. I'm sure I can get it to look a little better than it does now."

Great. Just what Robert needed. Another person taking a pair of scissors to his hair.

# Humiliated

In the morning, Robert searched his closet for a hat he could wear to school. All he could find was a pirate's hat that he'd worn in a class play in second grade. That wouldn't do the trick. It would just make everyone notice him even more. He thumped down the stairs.

Charlie came bounding down the stairs behind him. "Yo, Rob," he said, tossing his Yankees baseball cap to him as he passed by. "So long," he shouted as the door slammed after him.

Mrs. Dorfman shook her head as Robert entered the kitchen and grabbed a glass of orange juice. "I wish you boys would eat a decent breakfast before school."

Robert hardly heard what she said. He looked at the baseball cap. Charlie could be really nice sometimes. He put on the hat and ran out the door.

"Robert!" his mom shouted after him. But Robert was already on his way to meet Paul.

When they got to school, Robert left the cap on.

"Wouldn't you feel more comfortable taking off your cap, Robert?" asked Mrs. Bernthal.

"Um, no, I would rather wear it," said Robert. He slid down in his seat.

"Well, all right," said Mrs. Bernthal. "You may keep it on, if it means so much to you. I'm not a baseball fan myself, but I know how important it is to some of you."

"Yeah, right," said Matt. "Robert's a real sports fan." He giggled at his own joke. Everybody knew Robert was no athlete.

Except for Matt's remark, the rest of the morning went by without any teasing—until recess.

The boys were horsing around in the school yard. "Catch!" shouted Brian to Matt. Joey was in the middle, trying to get his hat back. As it sailed through the air toward Matt, Joey jumped up and caught it. Brian and Matt looked around for someone else to tease.

Before Robert knew it, Matt raced up and yanked his baseball cap off to continue the game. "Catch!" Matt shouted, tossing the cap to Brian.

Brian caught the cap and froze. "Look at Robert!"

"Holy cow!" said Matt.

"Robert! Where's your hair?" yelled Joey.

Robert had never felt so humiliated. The other kids gathered around to look at his hair—or what was left of it.

Paul came over. "It will grow back," he assured Robert. Good old Paul, to think of something thoughtful to say.

"Yeah," said Robert. He took the baseball cap from Brian, who stood there with his mouth open.

It was absolutely amazing how naked Robert felt without his hair.

# Sunset Pines

"Class, we're going to start a new project." Robert, still wearing Charlie's baseball cap, sat up straight to listen. He could use something to take his mind off his hair.

"The Sunset Pines Senior Home needs volunteers to run small errands for some of the residents. Would you like to help?" said Mrs. Bernthal.

"Yes!" said Vanessa Nicolini and Emily Asher at the same time.

"Me, me!" said Susanne Lee, raising her hand. Other hands went up, including Robert's.

"What kind of errands?" asked Lester Willis. Lester never raised his hand. He just shouted out whatever he had to say.

"Oh, buying a box of tissues or a ball of yarn. Something like that."

Robert's hand was still up. Mrs. Bernthal stuck a piece of paper in it as she went around the room. "You'll need your parents' permission to go," she said. "Please have them sign this form." Robert tucked his permission slip in his notebook.

After dinner, Robert called Paul on the telephone. "Did your parents say it's okay to go to Sunset Pines?" he asked.

"Yes. My mom thinks it's a good idea to help the old people. Why?"

"I was just thinking. What if they send us on an errand to get something gross?" said Robert.

"Like what?" asked Paul.

"Like false teeth cleaner," Robert said.

"Oh, yeah. Or corn pads. I guess we'll

just have to do it," said Paul. There was a pause. "As long as we don't have to try them out first."

Robert thought that was so funny he laughed until his sides hurt.

Friday finally came. At ten minutes of two, they left to board the school bus for the short trip to Sunset Pines. On the bus, Mrs. Bernthal reminded them of what they were to do.

"When you learn what your errand is, write it down," she said. Robert checked his pants pocket. He had a clean sheet of paper from his notebook, folded several times. A pencil was in his shirt pocket.

"You will have a week to do your errand. We will come back again next Friday," explained Mrs. Bernthal.

The nursing home had a big lobby. The walls were covered with pictures. Some were photographs of the residents at birthday parties. MRS. PITKIN, 90 YEARS OLD, read the label underneath one photo. Another said JANE GREELEY'S 82ND BIRTHDAY. Mrs. Pitkin and Jane Greeley looked very cute in their party hats.

A woman in a bright pink suit came out to greet them. First she introduced herself to Mrs. Bernthal. Then she turned to the children.

"Hello, children. I'm Mrs. Mooney." Mrs. Mooney used her hands when she spoke. "I want to thank you for helping our residents with their errands. We are very grateful to you." She held her arms out wide, as though she wanted to hug them all.

"Come on," she said, motioning them to follow her. She led them to the lounge, where a TV set played. No one was watching it. There were people sitting around on sofas and in easy chairs. A few were in wheelchairs. Robert had never seen so many people in wheelchairs before.

"What's wrong with them?" he whispered to Paul.

Paul shrugged. "I don't know," he whispered back.

As they went around the room, Mrs. Mooney introduced the children to the elderly residents.

Robert was assigned to Mrs. Santini, a lady with crinkly white curls. She sat in one of the wheelchairs.

"Ah, a Yankees fan," she remarked, seeing Robert's baseball cap.

"Hi," said Robert. "I really don't know much about baseball. This is my brother's cap."

"I don't know much about baseball, either," said Mrs. Santini, "but Mr. Santini was a Yankees fan, so I went with him to see some games. We always had a good time. And I saw Babe Ruth play!"

Robert was impressed. He had heard of the great Babe Ruth.

For her errand, Mrs. Santini asked Robert to buy her some candy. She handed him a dollar.

"What kind of candy?" he asked.

"Not hard candy," she said. "That's for old ladies." She winked. "I want something you have to chew. I may not have all my own teeth, but I have some. And they feed us only soft food here. I need to chew something."

For some reason, that made Robert think of Trudy's chew stick. He had a terrible urge to laugh. He turned quickly to look out the window until he could control himself.

When the time was up, Mrs. Bernthal asked them to say good-bye and get back on the bus. Robert felt a little sad. The whole time he was with Mrs. Santini, he hadn't thought once about his horrible hair.

# Seven Wonders

"**W**ho was your old person?" asked Paul as they rode back to school.

"Mrs. Santini. Who was yours?"

"Mrs. Levine," said Paul.

"What did Mrs. Levine want you to get for her?"

"A magnifying glass," said Paul.

"A magnifying glass?" asked Robert. "Why?"

"She says she needs it to look up telephone numbers in her address book. Her eyesight is not so good."

"Oh," Robert said. "I never thought of that. Mrs. Santini wants me to bring her candy. Chewy candy." He smiled when he remembered what Mrs. Santini had said about the soft food at Sunset Pines and how he'd thought of Trudy's chew stick.

"What's so funny?" asked Paul.

Robert told him. They began to laugh.

"Maybe she'd like one," said Paul.

Robert couldn't hold it in anymore. They got sillier and sillier, holding their sides laughing. It felt good to laugh, especially when you were nervous about something.

Robert had felt a little nervous being around all those people in wheelchairs. He felt sorry for them. He was also afraid, and he didn't know why.

"Do you think they are all sick?" he asked Paul.

"No. I think that when you get old, your legs just don't work so well anymore. It

happened to my gram. She uses a walker now. We see her all the time, and she comes over. When we go out and there's a lot of walking, she uses a wheelchair. But she's not sick."

That was good to hear. It made Robert wonder about Nana, his great-grandmother, who lived in Florida. He hadn't seen her in a long time. Maybe that was why. It would be hard to travel with a walker or a wheelchair.

Robert knew exactly what to bring Mrs. Santini. He bought her a Seven Wonders bar. It had seven different ingredients—chocolate, caramel, marshmallow, coconut, walnuts, raisins, and cherries. It was pretty chewy.

"This is just the thing," said Mrs. Santini on their next visit. She put the Seven Wonders bar in her pocket and handed the change back to Robert. "Thank you, but keep that for yourself."

"Thanks," said Robert.

He sat down in the chair next to the window. "Do you have any errands for next time?"

"Well, you can bring me another Seven Wonders bar," said Mrs. Santini, reaching into her pocket. She fished out another dollar and handed it to Robert. "If it ain't broke, don't fix it," she said with a twinkle in her eye.

Robert didn't really understand what Mrs. Santini meant, and besides, he was wondering how come she used the word "ain't." Mrs. Bernthal told them "ain't" was like choosing a word from the bottom of the barrel, when they had such beautiful ones they could use from the top.

As the bus chugged along the streets toward school, Robert realized what Mrs. Santini had meant. "If it ain't broke, don't fix it" meant "If you like something the way it is, don't change it." He laughed out loud. That was a pretty good saying.

# Just Ask

After a few visits to Sunset Pines, Robert's hair had begun to grow in. He didn't feel so weird anymore. He stopped wearing the Yankees cap.

"Robert? Is that you?" Mrs. Santini said as he walked in one Friday afternoon. "You look different."

Oh, no! Not again. "Really? How?" he squeaked.

"I've never seen you without your base-ball cap before," the old woman continued.

"Oh, that," said Robert. He smiled and

sat down. He pulled a Seven Wonders bar out of his jacket pocket and handed it to Mrs. Santini with her change. Again, she made him keep the change. Robert thanked her.

"What did you think I meant?" asked Mrs. Santini.

Robert was glad to tell someone. "On the first day of school a girl in my class said I looked different." Mrs. Santini was listening very carefully. Robert continued, "I couldn't figure out what she meant. I thought my hair looked funny and I ended up with a terrible, horrible, no good, very bad haircut." He used the line from a book he'd once read about a boy named Alexander who had a "terrible, horrible, no good, very bad day." Robert smiled. He had loved that book. He wondered if Mrs. Santini would like to read it. "But I'm still not sure if that's what she meant," Robert finished.

"Why don't you ask her?" said Mrs. Santini.

*Ask her?* Robert stared at Mrs. Santini. He had never thought of that. Why not? The worst that could happen is that Susanne Lee would laugh in his face and humiliate him. But he had already been humiliated.

That day, as he left Mrs. Santini, he had a big grin on his face. "See you next Friday!" he shouted. "And thanks!" He ran out to the bus.

"Susanne Lee!" he called. "Wait a minute!"

Susanne Lee spun around. "What?"

"I have to ask you something." Robert cleared his throat.

"Okay. Ask," said Susanne Lee.

"Remember what you said to me on the first day of school? About how I looked different?"

"Yes. So?"

"How?" asked Robert.

"How?" repeated Susanne Lee.

"Yes. How did I look different?"

Susanne Lee laughed out loud, just as Robert had expected she would. But it wasn't mean. "Robert, don't you know?" she said. "You must have had a growth spurt. You're so much taller. Can't you tell?"

"Um, no. I mean . . . sure. I . . . thanks. Thanks for telling me." Susanne Lee shrugged and got on the bus. Vanessa and Emily caught up to her, giggling.

Wow. Even with weird hair, Robert felt great. Imagine! Being taller was the best back-to-school special of all!